All Night Long

All Night Long

Emily Bunney

4 Horsemen
Publications, Inc.

All Night Long
Copyright © 2021-2024 Emily Bunney. All rights reserved.

4 Horsemen
Publications, Inc.

Published By: 4 Horsemen Publications, Inc.

4 Horsemen Publications, Inc.
PO Box 417
Sylva, NC 28779
4horsemenpublications.com
info@4horsemenpublications.com

Cover by Niki Tantillo

All rights to the work within are reserved to the author and publisher. No part of this publication may be reproduced, stored in a retrieval system, or transmitted in any form or by any means, electronic, mechanical, photocopying, recording, scanning, or otherwise, except as permitted under Section 107 or 108 of the 1976 International Copyright Act, without prior written permission except in brief quotations embodied in critical articles and reviews. Please contact either the Publisher or Author to gain permission.

All characters, organizations, and events portrayed in this novel are either products of the author's imagination or are used fictitiously.

All brands, quotes, and cited work respectfully belongs to the original rights holders and bear no affiliation to the authors or publisher.

Library of Congress Control Number: 2021941811

Audiobook ISBN: 978-1-64450-297-6
Ebook ISBN: 978-1-64450-298-3
Print ISBN: 978-1-64450-299-0

Dedication

For my good friends Nikki and Wendy. You're my girls and no matter how far apart we are, we'll always be together.

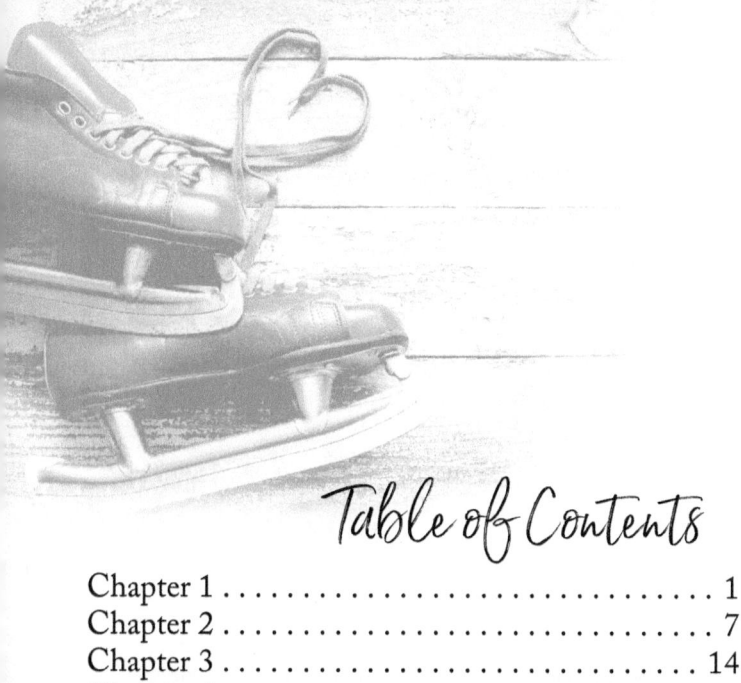

Table of Contents

Chapter 1 1
Chapter 2 7
Chapter 3 14
Chapter 4 20
Chapter 5 25
Chapter 6 31

*Find out what really happened the night
Cam and Bugs got together.*

Cameron

Shit, I'm late. I really hate being late for things. It's one of my little OCD quirks. Most of my friends are ten minutes late for everything, but I'm usually ten minutes early. I've never missed a flight or an appointment; the very thought gives me hives.

As I push my way through the double doors that lead into Matt Landon's new house, I hear the rumble of deep male voices. This is what I expect to hear since I'm entering a house full of NHL hockey players. However, the actual sound that assaults my ears is one similar to a bag of cats being drowned.

Is that supposed to be The Backstreet Boys?

Matt's housewarming/moving in with his girlfriend party is in full swing, and I soon realize that the horrible singing is due to the karaoke happening in the main room. I greet several of the players as I work my way toward the terrible singing, and before I know what's happening, a large, calloused hand grabs my wrist and pulls me into the commotion.

The hand belongs to the captain of the Seattle Whalers, Warren "Bugs" Parker, and he appears to be singing in my face.

"What the fuck, Warren?" I hiss as I try to look round his huge shoulders to see what's happening. However, Warren is determined to serenade me, moving his muscular body against me, his fern green eyes twinkling with mischief, his face split in half by that breathtaking grin.

As the song slows down, Warren turns and saunters away from me, and I get a clearer view of what's happening; I see the entire first line of the Whalers down on their knees in front of my good friend Beth. They continue to sing to her while our defenseman, Nate, holds her hand. I can see her light blue eyes are filled with tears, and she's smiling and nodding like a woman in love.

I see what this is all about—Nate has obviously roped in his pals to help him win Beth back. And it looks like it's working.

As the song picks up for the big finale, all the guys leap to their feet and begin to dance around like fools. I see Warren making a beeline for me again, and I try to back away into the crowd, but I feel several pairs of large hands pushing me forward. Before I can protest, I'm pulled into Warren's large arms and we're dancing. Actually, dancing isn't the right word; we're grinding against each other, and suddenly all I can see are his dazzling green eyes.

"Hey Cam," he whispers as his hands move down my back to the top of my ass.

Wow, Warren's hands are on my ass!

Cameron

It feels like all the air has been sucked out of the space, and it's just the two of us. We've been friends for years, and I thought I'd filed him securely in the Friend Zone. However, the way we're pressing against each other is definitely beyond friendly, and suddenly I'm unbelievably confused.

This is definitely a complication I don't need in my life at the moment. But it's been so long since I've been wanted and desired in the way I know Warren does—what harm can it do? I work hard so I have no time to date, and my last serious relationship was over a year ago.

Perhaps I can allow myself one little taste of this deliciously sexy man ... one little taste is all I need.

Suddenly, the music ends, and a huge cheer fills the room. I peek over Warren's massive shoulder and see Nate and Beth basically dry humping in front of everyone, kissing frantically. I guess it's safe to say she forgives him for dumping her at his mom's funeral.

Warren is still holding me tightly, his large hands still cupping my ass, and if I'm not mistaken there's a definite press of his cock against my hip. I swallow loudly and return my eyes to his, which are hooded and aroused. *Why doesn't this feel weird? Why am I getting wet with arousal at the hard press of my best friend's dick against me?* I'm sure he can feel the hammering of my heart against his chest, so I bring my hands up and firmly push him away. I need some distance so I can think. I don't need my pussy making any rash decisions in the heat of the moment!

Warren looks momentarily crestfallen at my rejection, but quickly it's replaced by his smirky grin.

"C'mon, Sawyer. Let's get a drink." He laughs. "I think we both need to obliterate that little display from our memories with lots of tequila."

I laugh as well, relieved that Warren isn't going to be weird about our little moment. I allow my best friend to take my hand, and he leads us through the crowd of players to the kitchen island that's literally groaning with bottles of liquor and glasses.

As Warren pours tequila into shot glasses, I push the feelings of arousal to the back of my mind. No matter how lonely and horny I am, sleeping with my best friend is not the answer. It would just be a complication that could ruin everything I've built here in Seattle.

Bugs

I pound the shot of tequila and welcome the smooth burn of the liquor. However, it does nothing to quench the thirst I have for my best friend. *I'm such a fucking idiot. Why did I grab Cam, of all people, to dance with during that ridiculous karaoke stunt?* I just couldn't help myself. I saw her coming in late to the housewarming party, and as I watched all the other guys grab a nearby lady, I went straight for her. It was like I had no control over myself when I pulled her into my arms and sang at her.

The look of shock and then annoyance on her sweet face made me chuckle as we danced together.

And I must admit, the feeling of her soft breasts and slim hips against me gave me instant wood.

"So what the hell was that all about?" Cam asks, pulling me back into the moment. "You guys are the worst singers I've ever heard."

I chuckle and pour us another shot which, to my surprise, Cam accepts. She's not known as a big drinker, and to be honest, she's a complete lightweight.

"Knox and Nate came up with this bonehead plan to win Beth back." I nod in the direction of the couple who are still kissing passionately against the fridge. "It looks like it worked."

Cam follows my gaze, her cheeks heat up to an adorable pink color, and I swear, for one second, I see a look of longing on her face. It quickly passes and she downs the shot, wincing slightly as she swallows.

"I'm glad they worked it out," she says wistfully, shaking her head and putting her palm over her shot glass as I try to pour another. "It must be nice to have that much passion with someone."

I snort out a laugh and pour myself another shot, probably my last, because I feel my tongue getting a little loose, and if I'm not careful, I'll be confessing all sorts to Cam. Most importantly, how I think we could have that much passion together if she gave us a chance.

"Hey, Cam! You made it." Thankfully, Mila chooses that moment to make an appearance and pulls Cam into a tight hug. "I'm so sorry Bugs did that to you." She slaps one of my thick biceps and scowls at me.

"Hey! I thought it was a fucking awesome performance," I scoff, rolling my eyes.

"Seriously dude, if hockey stops working for you, please DO NOT take up singing." Mila laughs, scrunching up her nose and reaching for Cam's hand. "Come on. Let me show you around."

Before I can protest, the girls disappear into the throng of bodies, and I'm left standing alone at the counter considering another shot.

Cameron

"Honestly, it was pretty hot," I confess to Beth and Mila as we sit on the massive California king in the master bedroom.

I notice my two friends sharing a look, and I curse the shots of tequila that have loosened my tongue.

"I knew you were hot for Bugs," Beth crows, smiling smugly.

"I'm not hot for him," I protest. "I said the situation was hot. I mean, I challenge any heterosexual woman to not feel something when a big, muscly man grinds up against her and feels her ass."

"He felt your ass?" They cry in unison, and I roll my eyes, burying my red face in my hands, and press my forehead to the comforter, mortified at my confession.

"Yes," I reply in a muffled voice.

"Well honey, if you want to take things to the next level with Bugs, I'd say tonight's the night," Beth says, guiding me back into a sitting position and pulling my hands away from my face.

"Don't pressure her!" Mila scolds. Then, fixing me with her whiskey-colored eyes, she asks, "*Do* you want that, Cam?"

"Ugh, I don't know. It's been over a year since Richard and I broke up, and I've been too busy to date," I explain.

"You know you don't have to date to get some, right?" Beth chuckles. "That's what Tinder's for. And if you don't get some D in your P soon, it'll grow over!"

"You're so nasty," Mila cries. "Thank god Nate's finally sealed the deal. I don't think there are any men left for you in Seattle."

Beth slaps her friend's thigh and sticks her tongue out. Beth was a wildly independent commitment-phobe until she finally gave her heart to the Whalers young defenseman.

"I don't do casual hookups. It's not my thing. It takes time for me to feel comfortable with someone I'm gonna sleep with," I explain.

"Well, that makes Bugs the perfect candidate!" Beth cries. "You're already best friends, so you *are* comfortable with him."

I laugh and shake my head. "It's a big step from being comfortable sitting in my sweats watching a rom-com with him to .. you know … letting him see all my stuff." I blush at the thought of Warren seeing me naked. But along with that comes a flash of heat at the thought of seeing him naked. All that hard muscle and ripped abs.

Wow!

I've seen plenty of Warren's body before: in swim trunks at Coach's annual Labor Day party and the odd times I've had to walk through the locker room with the GM after a game. But the prospect of seeing him naked and aroused makes my damp panties just a little bit wetter.

"You're totally thinking about it." Beth smirks, drawing me out of my erotic daydream.

"Am not," I grumble. "C'mon, let's see the rest of this palace." I stand up and head to the door, the possibility of actually sleeping with my best friend, just for one night, now at the forefront of my mind.

Bugs

"That's another hundred bucks you owe me," Thor bellows as he slaps his royal flush down on the green felt of the poker table.

"For fuck's sake, man," Matt grumbles, throwing his useless cards down with a huff. "Have you got x-ray vision or something?"

"Nope. Just naturally talented at everything I do." Our huge Swedish goalie jumps up from his chair and performs a victory dance that causes the rest of us to pelt him with chips and pretzels.

"Sit down, you dick." I laugh, sweeping the discarded cards toward me. "Another hand?"

"Nah, man. I'm gonna go find my woman." Matt stands and throws the cash he owes Thor onto the table, flips him off, and disappears to find Mila.

"Anyone else?" I ask around the table where Nate, Thor, and Ford sip their beers and munch on snacks. The karaoke is still going strong in the main room, and thankfully someone who can actually carry a tune is in charge of the mic.

"I'm getting another drink," Ford states in his smooth Tennessee drawl. "And then I'm gonna find me a hot woman to dance with."

All of us rise from the table, the game forgotten, and Thor and Ford head off in search of any available women while Nate and I move through the door to the kitchen.

"You and Cam looked cozy earlier," the kid states as we pick at the various snacks laid out on the table.

"I guess," I reply noncommittally, popping a chunk of cheese into my mouth, chewing slowly.

"Anything ever happened between you two?" he presses. Jesus, just because he's all loved up, he thinks he's an expert on this shit.

"Nah, man. She was with someone when we met, and by the time she was single, we were deep into the Friend Zone," I lie. I know Cam has *me* in the Friend Zone, but she certainly isn't as far as I'm concerned. I've wanted Cam in the worst way for years, but to be honest, I value her friendship more. Over the years, we've found we have a lot in common, so friendship seemed the sensible route to take to keep her in my life. But I won't lie—if that ever changes, I'll be all in.

"Speak of the devil," Nate whispers. "Incoming." He nods his head over my shoulder, and I turn to see Beth and Cam approaching.

"Here you are—near the food. Shocker!" Beth laughs, jumping into Nate's arms, wrapping her legs around him, kissing him deeply. "Did you eat a jalapeno popper?"

Cam and I both burst out laughing at the overshare, and Nate rolls his eyes.

"Princess, you know you don't have to say every crazy thing that comes into your head, right?" Nate chuckles, but she leans in and whispers something in his ear causing a red stain to color his cheeks.

"Okay, scrap that piece of advice. We're going to find an empty room."

And with that, Nate carries Beth away while she fistpumps the air and clings to him like a monkey.

Suddenly, I find myself alone with Cam in the kitchen, and the air between us seems to crackle with a strange new energy I've never felt before. If I'm not mistaken, she seems nervous and fidgety, picking at the bowl of pretzels beside her.

"Those two are insatiable." I chuckle, trying to break this weird tension between us. "I hope she doesn't break the kid. We need him for our Cup run this season."

That makes Cam laugh and blush as she tucks strands of silky brown hair behind her ear. My fingers are itching to do the same and much more, but I have to beat those feelings down. She doesn't want that from me, and I'm not going to be a douche about it and force myself on her.

But the next words out of her mouth leave me completely dumbfounded.

"Do you ever think about me like that?" she asks quietly, shyly flashing her dark brown eyes at me. I notice that her pupils are dilated and her breath seems to be coming out too quickly.

For a moment, I can't form words. I'm in complete shock. Cam's never asked me this before. I didn't think this was something she ever thought about. But now she's asked me the question, and I've left her hanging.

I can see the doubt creeping into her eyes the longer I stay silent. She's losing her nerve, and the longer I wait, the less chance I have of potentially getting what I've always wanted.

I need to show her just how much I want her, so I step up to her and cup her face in my hands. Jesus, her skin is soft and warm and just being this close to her has me hardening in my jeans. I fix her brown eyes with mine and smile.

"Of course I have, Sawyer." I confess in a quiet, rough voice. She looks relieved and a little turned on, her chin quivering, which is a sign she's getting emotional. "You know how I feel about you, but I've respected your decision to just be friends. But if you need more, I'm here."

Cam averts her eyes for a moment, and I just pray no one comes in and breaks the spell we're under. I can see the struggle she's having in her head: sensible Cam versus the passionate woman I know she keeps under wraps. She draws her plump bottom lip between her teeth, and I become fully hard, my dick pressing into my zipper. If she doesn't speak soon, I'm just going to kiss her. *To hell with it.*

Then her eyes come back to mine, and I see the determination in them. Her words confirm what I hope I see.

"I need you, Warren," she says in a raspy, aroused voice, and my world lights up like the Fourth of July. "Just for tonight ... please." And just as quickly, I'm plunged into darkness. She just wants a one-night thing, so we can scratch this itch we seem to have for each other. Obviously, I want more with her, but if this is what she needs, I'll be there for her.

I drop my hands from her face and take her hand. "Let's get out of here," I growl.

3

Cameron

Why the hell did Matt have to buy a house in the middle of nowhere?

This journey is the longest of my life, and as I follow Warren in his SUV, I consider chickening out at every turn we pass. It would be so easy to turn off the road, forget this stupid idea, and go home to my cat. I know it would be the sensible thing to do, especially if Warren and I want to continue to be friends. But my libido has other plans. When Warren literally dragged me out of the party, my pussy flooded and my nipples hardened at the growly alpha he became. I had no idea I found that kind of behavior attractive; all my previous boyfriends had been very considerate, gentle lovers, sensible boys with glasses and sweater vests. Richard had worked for a non-profit, and I thought he wanted to save the world. That is until I found out he was a cheating snake. However, the thought of Warren taking me in a rough, passionate way has me following him all the way to his house.

Cameron

I pull up behind his Range Rover and turn off the engine of my Jeep. I have to take a moment to control my breathing and fend off the panic rising in my chest. *What the hell am I doing?* This is not like me at all. I'm not the girl who randomly hooks up with people. I don't even know how to do this.

Suddenly, my door opens and Warren's standing there, smiling and holding his hand out to me. "You gonna sit out here all night, or are you coming in? No pressure."

And just those two words remind me I'm not going home with some random guy I've met at a club. I'm with my best friend, and I know he'll never do anything to hurt me or make me uncomfortable. If I call this off right now and suggest a sappy movie and popcorn, he'll go with it.

So, I take a deep breath, pull up my imaginary big girl pants, and take his hand, sliding out of the Jeep to stand before him.

"Are you totally sure about this, Sawyer? There really is no pressure …" Warren begins, but I reach up and cover his mouth with my palm.

"Yes I'm sure, and I don't wanna talk about it anymore." I swallow hard and will myself to say what I need. "I need you to kiss me and take me inside, take me to your bed, and fuck me."

I see the momentary shock in Warren's eyes at my crass words, but that's soon replaced by a fire I've never experienced before. His eyes are now a dark green, and he licks his lips before leaning down to capture my mouth gently. His lips feel incredible, warm and soft but with a firm pressure that lights me up. I tilt my head slightly, inviting him to deepen the kiss, and soon his tongue runs along the seam of my mouth, and I open for him. I tentatively touch my tongue to his, a deep moan rumbles up from his chest, and that sound alone turns me on. As we continue to explore each other's mouths, Warren presses me against the side of my Jeep, and I clearly feel the hard rod that was suggested when he danced earlier. Wow, he's huge, and I feel a small wave of panic again.

But before that can settle, Warren ends our kiss. "Let's go inside. If we don't, I might end up fucking you against your car," he growls, taking my hand again, pulling me toward his house. He quickly types in the door code, and we enter the dark foyer, coming together again in a passionate desperate way. Warren lifts me against him and kicks the door shut, carrying me upstairs while I plunder his mouth. He fists the hair at the nape of my neck and holds me firmly against him while my long legs lock around his waist.

I don't even recognize this wanton woman I appear to be when I'm with him. Just like the gentle, considerate lovers I've chosen in the past, I've never been one to lose control like this. It's always been nice, and I've had my fair share of orgasms, but this feels totally different. It feels like we could lose ourselves in each other, and that's a little bit scary.

However, I don't have time to consider this because Warren is marching like a man on a mission toward his huge bed, and we're falling onto the soft comforter, still locked together.

Bugs

I need to get my shit together, or I'm likely to bust a nut like a virgin on prom night. I still can't get my head around the fact that Cam is in my bed, beneath me, devouring me like I'm her last meal. I must admit I'm a bit shocked. I knew being with Cam would be amazing, but the passion and fire she has is unexpected. Not that I mind, I fucking love this version of Cam. It's making me so hard, I feel like my dick's about to punch through my zipper, especially when she slides her tongue against mine and palms my cock.

"Fuck me, Sawyer." I groan, reaching for her wrist. "You keep that up, and I'm gonna embarrass myself."

She chuckles, a deep throaty sound that makes my balls draw up, ready for release, and I have to start running Stanley Cup winning teams through my head to stop myself from coming.

"C'mon now, Cap. Don't let a girl down," she whispers in my ear, nibbling on the shell. "All I hear from Beth and Mila is how much stamina you hockey boys have. I need to see for myself."

I pull away, rising up on my elbow so I can look her straight in the eyes. "Challenge accepted." I whisper. "I'm gonna fuck you all night long, I'm gonna make you come so many times, you'll forget your own name."

Cam draws in her breath, and her already pink cheeks flush with arousal. "Wow," she gasps. "No one's ever used dirty talk with me before."

Suddenly, I'm worried I've pushed her too far.

But Cam nibbles her lower lip and looks at me coyly. "I like it."

Thank god. I love telling a woman what I want to do to her, what I want her to do to me, what I love about her body.

"That's good then." I chuckle. "Let's get some of these clothes off you. I wanna worship those perky tits of yours. I'm dying to know what color your nipples are and what they taste like."

Cam giggles as I pull her shirt over her head, taking her lace bralette along with it. As she lies down again, I'm greeted with the sight of her tits, a perfect handful topped with light brown nipples that are pebbled and hard. Before I can think, I latch my lips around one and draw it between my teeth, causing Cam to buck beneath me, grinding herself against my thigh.

Fuck, she's so responsive. The deep moans and desperate keening noises she makes as I work her nipples are sending me hurtling toward the precipice, and I need to slow this down. So I pull away and drag my own shirt over my head, throwing it behind me, reaching for the button on Cam's jeans. I flick it open and slowly drag the zipper down, keeping my eyes locked on hers. I want to memorize every look, every sound she makes as I bring her pleasure. If this is our only night, then I'm committing everything to my permanent collection.

As I drag her tight jeans over her hips and down her thighs, I pull off her boots and socks so I can remove them completely. Then Cam is lying on my bed wearing only a pair of impossibly small lace panties. She rises up on her elbows and drags her eyes down my bare chest to the buckle of my belt, the very obvious tent of my erection clearly visible.

"Your turn," she says, licking her lips and darting her eyes to my belt buckle.

I chuckle and undo my belt, pulling my jeans over my ass and down my thighs. "You're not how I expected you to be, Sawyer," I say as I toe off my sneakers and socks before joining her on the bed again, both of us just in our underwear.

She turns toward me and tentatively reaches out to graze her fingertips down my chest and over the ridges of my abs, her eyes drinking in everything with eager curiosity.

"What do you mean?" she asks, never looking up from tracing the journey of her fingers.

"I don't know. I guess I have no idea what you'd be like in bed." I shrug.

Suddenly, her eyes are locked on mine, and there's concern and embarrassment there.

"Am I being weird?" Her chin quivers, and I feel like an asshole for denting her confidence.

I take her heart-shaped face in my hands. "Look at me, Cam. You're passionate and sexy and everything you're doing is fucking incredible. I've never wanted anyone more than I want you right now."

And before she can speak or doubt herself more, I press my lips to hers in a searing kiss.

4

Cameron

"Oh ... oh ... oooohhhhhhh," I moan as I watch Warren's face press against my center, his eyes sliding closed in pleasure. All the sassy bravado I had going on has completely left the building, and I'm literally a molten pool of arousal. The rough scratch of his whiskers against my inner thighs tickles at first, and I let out a breathy giggle, but soon that feeling is surpassed by the insistent rhythm of his tongue. He strokes my hard clit over and over again, in a maddening tempo that's likely to make me come at record speed. *Who knew he'd be so fucking good at this?*

I reach down and grab a handful of his dark hair, pressing his face against me until I find just the right angle and pressure. My loud moan causes Warren to up his game, working me over like a man possessed.

"That's it, baby," he growls, lifting his head to look at me. "I want you to come all over my face."

Fuck me, his filthy words make my pussy clench, and a fresh wave of arousal makes me even wetter. Warren returns his lips and tongue to my center, but this time he adds in a couple of fingers, sliding them into my tight, wet channel.

His moan of appreciation tells me he likes what he finds, and as I grab his hair again to find that perfect angle, I spread my legs wide and buck my hips up to meet his mouth.

"That's it ... just there ... ooooohhhhhhh god!" I come so hard my toes curl and the joints crack, the muscles in my thighs quivering around Warren's face. He works me to the very last throb of my orgasm, only sitting up when I become too sensitive and have to push him away.

"That was so hot, Sawyer." He laughs breathlessly, wiping my cum from his mouth and chin. "You came like a fucking champ."

"Oh god," I moan breathlessly, covering my red, sweaty face with my arm. "Can you not call me Sawyer when we're doing this? Because every time you say it in the future, I'm likely to get turned on."

Warren stands up in front of me and pulls down his boxer briefs, his large thick cock springing free. "Perhaps that's my evil plan. It'll be like a Pavlovian response you just can't help."

I drag my eyes from staring at Warren's impressive dick and marvel at the fact that my hockey playing best friend knows what a Pavlovian response is.

"You're just full of surprises, aren't you?" I laugh as he lowers his massive, wide body down onto mine. I've been worried about this. He's so big I've been afraid he'll crush me. But instead of feeling suffocated, he feels like a living weighted blanket, and it's comforting and arousing all at once. I mean, if tiny Beth can manage with six foot seven Nate, then I can cope with Warren.

"I did go to college, you know. I'm not a dumb jock," he replies, trying hard to look offended but smirking at the same time.

"I know that," I whisper. "Talking of smart, do you have a condom?"

"Yes, ma'am." Warren leans down and kisses my nose, an oddly intimate gesture that makes my heart flutter in my chest. As he digs around in the nightstand for a condom, I remind myself that this is not the time to catch feelings for this man. Yes, he's sexy, kind, and funny, but a relationship between us would just be too complicated.

Warren quickly rolls the condom down his length and lies on his back next to me. I'm momentarily confused, but then he looks over at me and says, "I want you on top. I want to watch you ride my cock."

I gasp, again turned on by his dirty words. I've never really been an "on top" kind of girl, but I feel completely safe and confident with Warren. So I roll over and crawl over his large body, straddling his thighs so his cock is nestled against my mound. I wish I'd got to feel him in my mouth before he put the condom on, but he said we'd be at this all night long, so there's time to do all the naughty things that are suddenly coming to mind.

I do, however, wrap my hand around his cock, giving him an exploratory squeeze. Warren sucks in his breath and closes his eyes. He looks like it's almost painful, but when I move to take my hand away, he covers my hand with his.

Cameron

"You can hold me tighter if you want, but I'm really close, baby. So you might want to have at it," he groans, holding my hips, urging me to rise up on my knees.

I press my palms down on his hard abs to keep my balance as he guides me to the right angle to notch the head of his cock against my wet entrance. We both gasp as the first few inches slide inside me. It's been over a year since I had sex, so to begin with it's a little uncomfortable. Warren is stretching me so I have to pause to allow myself to get used to his size, my thighs quivering at the effort of holding still. Once I'm comfortable, I lower myself farther, inch by glorious inch, until Warren is fully sheathed inside me.

"Oh baby, you feel so good," Warren groans, his fingertips digging into my hips. "You're so tight and wet. You'll need to go slow to start."

I can't find the words to agree, I'm so turned on, so I just nod my head and begin to slowly rise and fall. I set a rhythm that causes my thigh muscles scream in protest: up, down, up, down, my palms plastered to his abs to help me.

"That's it, Cam. You can go faster now," Warren growls, grabbing my ass cheeks, his hips thrusting up off the mattress, meeting my downward strokes. I can feel the base of his thick cock rubbing against my swollen clit, and my orgasm is fast approaching but still maddeningly distant. As if sensing my need, Warren slides his calloused finger between my wet folds and rubs my nub, increasing the pressure until I throw my head back and cry out. The orgasm that rips through me feels like nothing I've ever had before; the fullness of Warren inside me, being squeezed by my spasms is incredible. It seems to last for an eternity, and just as I'm coming down, I feel Warren swell further inside me. He pulls me down onto his chest, flips me onto my back, grabs the back of my knee to lift my leg and pounds into me so hard, I begin to come again.

As I cry out, I reach down and grab his butt, pulling him in deep as we both freeze in our releases. Warren buries his face in my neck and sucks the skin there, causing me to yelp and squirm.

We lie together afterward, coming down from the ceiling, a tangle of sweaty limbs and heaving chests. As I come back to myself, I have a sudden worry that this will very quickly become awkward. But when Warren rises up and presses his firm lips to mine, his tongue gently stroking, those worries pass. He pushes my damp hair off my face and looks at me with a serious expression on his face.

"I don't want this to be awkward, so I'm gonna say this now before I lose my nerve."

Oh god, he's going to say this was a mistake. He's going to say he doesn't want to be friends anymore.

But Warren swallows and says, "This is the best time I've ever had, Sawyer. I just want you to know that." I can see his eyes shining with emotion even as tears sting my nose and the back of my throat. He's my best friend, and his words mean everything to me.

"It was for me too," I reply, leaning up to kiss him softly. "It was everything I needed tonight."

Bugs

"**D**o you want salt or butter?" I call from the kitchen as I rummage through the cupboard, looking for the microwave popcorn I keep stashed away for movie nights.

"Do you have sweet?" Cam calls back. "Can you make salted and sweet and mix them together?"

I chuckle to myself and shake my head, finding packets of salted and sweet. I should have known she'd ask for that; it's Cam's go-to popcorn mix. If she's feeling extra saucy, she asks me to add M&Ms as well. I think it's a bit gross, but she likes it that way. And at this moment, standing in my kitchen in a pair of low-slung athletic shorts while my best friend lounges on the couch in one of my hockey jerseys, I'm happy to give her whatever she wants. The sex we've just had was the best of my life. If I was with a casual hook up, I'd want her out of my place as soon as possible so I could go and hang out with Cam. But this is the best of both worlds—mindblowing sex and getting to hang with my friend.

The microwave pings, and I snatch the hot bag out, ripping it open and pouring the contents into a large bowl along with the first bag. Then I pour the M&Ms in and give the bowl a shake to mix it up. She may be my best friend, but her taste in snacks sucks.

Once I grab two sodas from the fridge, I head back into the main room to find Cam sprawled on the couch, surfing through my Netflix watch list.

"You really have the shittiest taste in movies." She laughs as I plop down next to her, handing her the bowl of mixed popcorn.

"And you have the shittiest taste in snacks. You're point being?" I ask, cocking an eyebrow at her, a smirk on my face.

Cam huffs out a breath, causing her messed up hair to fly around her face. "I'm just saying," she mutters. "It's all gangsters and war movies."

"It's better than the sentimental shit you always wanna watch," I reply, reaching to snatch the remote from her hand. But damn she's fast, switching it to the hand farthest from me and holding it out of my reach.

"Hey, c'mon now. This is my house. I get to choose what we watch," I growl, reaching across her, momentarily distracted by the fact that the jersey she's wearing is riding up her thighs, dangerously close to showing me whether or not she put her panties back on.

"Nuh uh," she tsks. "I think you'll find it's my choice tonight." Cam rolls away from me so my front is pressing against her back, and suddenly I'm not interested in what we watch on Netflix. I can feel my dick hardening against her butt, and I want to be inside her again.

Cam continues to squirm away from me, but as my arousal becomes more evident, she stops and looks over her shoulder, eyes wide with shock.

"Warren! You have a boner!" she gasps, her cheeks pink with embarrassment.

I laugh at how unbelievably cute she is and press myself against her ass even harder. "You better believe it, baby," I growl in her ear. "You keep squirming like that, and I'm gonna take you again right now."

Cam lets out a shaky breath and pushes back against me, causing me to groan and rest my forehead between her shoulder blades.

"What if I want that?" she asks quietly.

Oh, this night just gets better and better.

"Then I say you can have whatever you want, baby," I reply, planting a kiss on her hot cheek and sitting back, my long muscular arms stretching out along the back of the couch.

Slowly, Cam turns around and places the bowl of forgotten popcorn on the coffee table, her eyes burning with desire. She swallows and licks her lips, her eyes darting across my bare chest and abs. The shorts I'm wearing are doing nothing to hide my arousal.

"I ... want you ... in my mouth," she says quietly, nibbling on her plump lower lip.

I can't help but huff out a breath as my eyebrows shoot up my forehead. "Fuck, Sawyer." I run my hand through my messed-up hair. "Go for it."

Suddenly, Cam seems to lose her confidence when I hand over the reins to her. She looks unsure of where to start, so I help her out by lifting my ass off the couch and sliding my shorts down to my ankles, my hard dick springing free. Cam's eyes widen, and she licks her lips again, making my length twitch as her hands tentatively run up my muscular thighs.

"What do you want me to do?" she asks quietly. "How do you like it?"

God, she's so adorable, I want to sweep her into my arms and take charge, but I know that Cam needs to feel like she's getting this right.

"Anything you do will be perfect, baby." But I decide to give her a few pointers anyway. "I like firm, constant pressure, and I'm most sensitive around the head and along the vein on the underside. No need to try and deep throat me, but I do like to be held tightly around the base until I'm ready to come. Do you want a warning?"

Cam cocks her head to the side, and her eyebrows draw together. "A warning?"

"You know, before I ... come," I reply.

Cam giggles and shuffles closer, so she's on her knees between my thighs, her lip still clamped between her teeth. When it springs free, she licks it and looks at me with a burning desire that makes my balls draw up slightly. As she begins to lean into me, I quickly reach out and cup her face in my hands.

"Cam, you don't ..." I begin, but she shakes her head.

"I want to ... so much," she breathes. "Please kiss me first."

Damn, how can I resist that? Still holding her face gently in my hands, I lean forward and press my lips to hers, her tongue seeking mine out, sliding and tangling. She moans softly and grips my thick wrists, prolonging the kiss until I pull away and lean back against the couch cushions. I fist my rock-hard cock and give it a few pulls, enjoying the way Cam's eyes widen again, her lips swollen from our kisses.

For a second, I think she's just going to watch me jerk off, but then she surprises me by leaning forward and running her tongue up the underside of my dick, from root to tip, taking the head into her mouth.

"Fuck, Sawyer," I gasp, my hips arching off the couch making my dick slide deeper into her hot, wet mouth. Cam firmly presses my hips back down, so I slip out of her mouth slightly. Then she really goes to town, swirling her tongue around the head and gripping me firmly at the base, just like I instructed.

Pretty soon, she falls into a firm, constant rhythm, her head bobbing up and down in my lap, her wet lips suctioning me in and out. It feels fucking fantastic, and I can't help the panting breaths and deep rumbling moans that keep slipping from me as I get closer to my release.

As Cam continues to go down on me like a fucking champ, I notice her shift slightly, and the hand that isn't holding my dick disappears between her legs.

"Are you touching your pussy while you blow me, baby?" I growl, lightly brushing her silky brown hair out of her face, her eyes locking with mine. By way of reply, she groans around my dick, and the vibrations send a shiver of pleasure through me.

"Oh Jesus," I chuckle gruffly, my head falls back on the couch as she picks up the pace with both her mouth and her hand. Pretty soon, we're both moaning in unison, hurtling toward our climaxes.

"That's it, Sawyer. I want you to come with me. Finger your clit so you get there."

Cam moans around my dick again. I notice her hips are bucking in time with the bobbing action, and I know she's close. I sure as hell am.

"Baby, I'm gonna come," I grind out through gritted teeth. "If you don't want to swallow, you need to move and finish me with your hand."

I feel Cam give a determined shake of her head, and she seems to double her efforts to get us both off. And it doesn't take more than a few more strokes of her tongue and lips before I'm exploding in her mouth, my hips flexing, my hand fisting her hair. This action seems to trigger Cam's own climax, her mouth opening to release my dick as she moans and squeezes her eyes shut. As I come down, I notice some of my cum has escaped from her mouth, so I reach out and sweep it away with my thumb, sliding the thick digit into her mouth. She moans and sucks the fluid from it, releasing it with a wet pop.

"Hey, don't I get a taste?" I ask, loving the slightly shocked expression that sweeps across Cam's flushed face, making me laugh. "I don't wanna taste me. I wanna taste you," I clarify.

Still looking confused, I help her out by reaching down, grabbing Cam's hand and sliding her index and middle fingers into my mouth. I moan and roll my eyes in pleasure at the salty, tangy taste of her pussy, sucking her long fingers clean.

"I had no idea you were so nasty." Cam giggles, shaking her head. When I release her fingers from my mouth, I pull her up into my lap and kiss her deeply, sharing the taste of her pussy with her.

"You've got no idea," I growl against her lips. "Now, what that hell are we gonna watch on Netflix?"

6

Cameron

Who'd have thought going down on my best friend could be so hot? I've given head before, plenty of times with previous partners, but I've never been so desperate to do it as I was tonight. I just had to have Warren in my mouth, and it was so incredible, I got so turned on I had to finger myself to ease the throbbing ache in my pussy.

After he sucked the juices from my slick fingers and pulled me into his lap, we shared a searing kiss. I don't think I'll ever get tired of kissing him. But even as that thought enters my head, I realize that I will have to give up kissing Warren after tonight, and that thought makes me ache inside.

I slowly end the kiss and slide off Warren, allowing him to pull his shorts up while I take a swig of my warm soda. I suddenly feel like I want to run from our sexy little bubble before I get in any deeper.

"Everything okay?" Warren asks quietly, running his fingers down my arm, causing goosebumps to break out on my flushed skin.

Damn my traitorous body.

"Yeah, it's all good," I reply with false cheeriness, reaching for the popcorn and the remote. "How about *Anchorman*?" I suggest, desperate for a distraction from these confusing feelings.

Warren gives me one of his incredible smiles and pulls me into his side, his hand possessively gripping my hip. "Sounds perfect." He kisses the top of my head as I hit play, and we settle into the movie. I have to admit, it feels nice that we can still do this even after all the other extra-curricular activities we've engaged in tonight. My biggest fear is that things get awkward between us once this night is over and I lose the best friend I've ever had. I know I have Mila and Beth now, but I share something so special with Warren, and if we were to lose that, I'd be devastated.

As the movie plays out, I remember to laugh in all the right places, but my mind can't stop playing out all the scenarios of how things will go once we return to the real world of hockey, work, and friends. I know for a fact I don't want this to affect Warren's hockey career or my position within the franchise. Suddenly, this little tryst that seemed so simple when I propositioned him at the party could now have much wider implications for both of us.

"That was fun." Warren's deep voice draws me out of my reverie, and I notice the credits to the movie are rolling. *Where the hell did two hours go?*

"Huh?" I ask, looking up at him.

"You've been a million miles away, baby," he replies quietly, pressing his finger to my forehead. "Where'd you go?" I can see the concern creasing his brow, and it breaks my heart to think I've caused him worry or pain.

Cameron

But I decide that I need to be honest. I owe him that much as my best friend.

"I'm worried this will mess up our friendship," I explain quietly, lowering my eyes to watch my fingers fiddle with a loose thread on the hem of the jersey.

Warren's jersey.

I know what it means to wear it. I've seen both Mila and Beth claimed by their men this way. *Is that what Warren was doing when he gave it to me to wear? Or was this the first clean shirt he picked up?*

I'm so confused.

"Sawyer, look at me." Warren's fingers come up to my chin, and they lift my face so I'm looking into his fern green orbs. He has the most incredible eyes, deep green with long dark lashes that perfectly frame them. Sexy eyes. Kind eyes.

"You are one of the most important people in my life. You know that, right?" he demands, his voice raspy with emotion.

I can feel the sting of tears in my nose, so I just nod my acknowledgement.

"I know my feelings for you have always been bubbling beneath the surface. I'm not gonna lie—being with you tonight, like this, hasn't done anything to diminish them." He gently kisses my nose and smooths my cheeks with his thumbs. "But I'm happy going back to being friends with no benefits if that's what you want."

The adorable hopefulness in his eyes just about rips my heart out, but I know exactly what I have to do.

"I think that would be best. Going back to the way we were." I shrug and set my mouth in a hard line to stop my chin from quivering with emotion, averting my eyes from his again.

But Warren lifts my face, so I have nowhere to hide. I have to look at him, and I can see him trying to push his pain and disappointment down into his gut so as not to hurt me.

"If that's what you want, baby, that's what we'll do." He leans down and kisses my lips this time. "But for the rest of the night, it's just you and me. No Whalers, no friends, no expectations. Just you and me, Sawyer."

As much as I want to flee so I can protect both our hearts from further damage, I can't seem to move from the safety and warmth of his embrace. Our lips find each other again, moving slowly, deeply, and soon Warren's hands are searching for the hem of the jersey I'm wearing, seeking my bare skin. We slowly sink down onto the couch, Warren's weight on top of me, his hands on my body, his lips on my neck. And with agonizing slowness, he slides two thick fingers inside me, finding that spot that makes me gasp and mewl. My eyes fill with tears that slide silently down my cheeks.

"Take me to bed, Warren," I beg breathlessly, needing one last time with him. "Make love to me … please."

I feel his lips smile against mine, and quicker than I thought possible, Warren is up off the couch, and I'm sailing over his shoulder with a yelp of surprise.

"Put me down!" I squeal as he slaps my bare ass and carries me back to his bedroom.

"Not a chance, baby. You're mine for the next few hours, so I'm gonna make the most of it."

And my god, he does just that. He makes me come so many times I lose count. By the time we fall asleep wrapped in each other's arms, I'm sated and boneless. However, the dull ache in my chest grows steadily stronger as I watch Warren's sleeping face snuggled against my breasts.

I know that once dawn breaks, the magic spell we're under will vanish, and life will carry on as if this never happened.

But I'm not so sure I'll be able to forget about it that easily. In fact, I know I won't, and that fucking terrifies me.

Thankfully, I'm so exhausted that sleep soon takes me, and I drift off, safe in Warren's embrace for probably the last time.

Bugs

For as long as I've known Cameron, I've wanted her. And tonight, I finally got what I needed, what I craved. Sure, I've been happy in the Friend Zone if it meant we could hang out, but the deep, throbbing need to get my hands on her curves has been a daily obsession.

Looking down at her sweet, sleeping face fills me with so much emotion it makes my chest hurt. I'm not going to lie. The caveman inside is beating his chest and wants to shout about his conquest from the rooftops. But along with that, there's a protectiveness that makes me want to hold her to me, to be all she needs.

Obviously, I'm sated after the incredible sex we've just had. She was so uninhibited which surprised me. Cam has always had a gentle, kind nature, except when she's at work, then she's all business. When she gave me that sizzling look at Matt and Mila's housewarming party and told me she wanted me, I couldn't get us out of there fast enough.

Part of me knew this could ruin our friendship forever, but that part wasn't in charge as her soft, full lips crashed against mine. I couldn't think straight as I gripped her slim hips and guided her movements on top of me. And my mind was completely blown when she came apart beneath me, moaning and writhing in so much pleasure it caused me to release with such power I saw stars.

Cam shifts in my arms and snuggles in deeper, hooking her long leg over mine, but she doesn't wake. I can feel my eyelids drooping and the steady rhythm of her breathing is lulling me to sleep. However, I don't want to miss a second of this time with her. If this is it, if this one incredible night is all I get, then I'm going to hold on to each precious moment.

This is the last thought I have before sleep finally claims me.

And when I wake the next morning, I'm alone.

Read the rest of Bugs and Cam's story in All She Needs!

Discover more at
4HorsemenPublications.com

10% off using HORSEMEN10

www.ingramcontent.com/pod-product-compliance
Lightning Source LLC
LaVergne TN
LVHW042004060526
838200LV00041B/1865